KT-152-813

Diary of a Wombat

written by
Jackie French

illustrated by
Bruce Whatley

Angus&Robertson
An imprint of HarperCollins Children's Books

Angus&Robertson
An imprint of HarperCollins*Children'sBooks* Australia

First published in Australia in 2002
This edition published in 2013
by HarperCollins*Publishers* Australia Pty Limited
ABN 36 009 913 517
harpercollins.com.au

Text copyright © Jackie French 2002
Illustrations copyright © Introspective Bear 2000

The rights of Jackie French and Bruce Whatley to be identified as the author
and illustrator of this work have been asserted by them in accordance with
the *Copyright Amendment (Moral Rights) Act 2000.*

This book is copyright. Apart from any use as permitted under the *Copyright Act 1968,* no part
may be reproduced, copied, scanned, stored in a retrieval system, recorded or transmitted,
in any form or by any means, without the prior written permission of the publisher.

HarperCollins*Publishers*
Level 13, 201 Elizabeth Street, Sydney, NSW 2000, Australia
Unit D1, 63 Apollo Drive, Rosedale, Auckland 0632, New Zealand
1 London Bridge Street, London SE1 9GF, United Kingdom
A 53, Sector 57, Noida, UP, India
2 Bloor Street East, 20th floor, Toronto, Ontario M4W 1A8, Canada
195 Broadway, New York NY 10007, USA

National Library of Australia Cataloguing-in-Publication data:

French, Jackie.
    Diary of a wombat.
    ISBN 978 0 2071 9995 0 (hbk.)
    ISBN 978 0 2071 9836 6 (pbk.)
    For children.
    1. Wombats – Juvenile literature. I. Whatley, Bruce. II.Title.
599.24

Bruce Whatley used acrylic paints to create the illustrations for this book
Cover and internal design by HarperCollins Design Studio
Colour reproduction by Graphic Print Group, Adelaide
Printed in China by RR Donnelley on 128gsm Matt Art

28 27   18 19 20

To Mothball, and all the others.
JF

Thanks for letting me play, Jackie.
This was fun.
BW

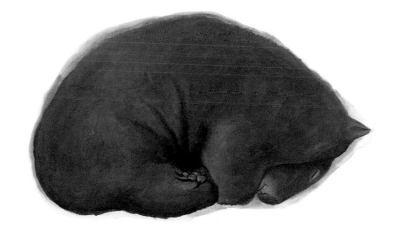

Monday

Morning: Slept.

Afternoon: Slept.

Evening: Ate grass.

Scratched.

Night: Ate grass.

Slept.

Tuesday

Morning: Slept.

Afternoon: Slept.

Evening: Ate grass.

Night: Ate grass. Decided grass is boring.

Scratched. Hard to reach the itchy bits.

Slept.

Wednesday

Morning: Slept.

Afternoon: Mild cloudy day.

Found the perfect dustbath.

Discovered flat, hairy creature
invading my territory.

Fought major battle with
flat, hairy creature.

Won the battle.

Demanded a carrot.

The carrot was delicious.

Evening: Demanded more carrots.

No response.

Chewed hole in door.

FOR PETE'S SAKE,
GIVE HER SOME
CARROTS!

Ate carrots.
Scratched.
Went to sleep.

Thursday

Morning: Slept.

Afternoon:

Discovered the perfect scratching post.

Evening: Demanded carrots.
No response.
Tried yesterday's hole.
Curiously resistant to my paws.

Bashed up garbage bin
till carrots appeared.

Ate carrots.

Began new hole in soft dirt.

Went to sleep.

Friday

Morning: Slept.

Afternoon: Discovered new
scratching post.

Also discovered a new source of carrots.

Evening: Someone has filled in my new hole.

Soon dug it out again.

Night: Worked on hole.

Saturday

Morning: Moved into new hole.

Afternoon: Rained.

New hole filled up with water.

Moved back into old hole.

Evening: Discovered even more carrots.
Never knew there were so many carrots in the world.
Carrots delicious.

Night: Finished carrots.
Slept.

Sunday

Morning: Slept.

Afternoon: Slept.

Evening: Slept.

Night: Offered carrots at the back door.

Why would I want carrots when I feel like rolled oats?
Demanded rolled oats instead. Humans failed
to understand my simple request.
Am constantly amazed how dumb humans can be.

Chewed up one pair of boots, three cardboard boxes,
eleven flower pots and a garden chair
till they got the message.

Ate rolled oats.

Scratched. Went to sleep.

Monday

Morning: Slept.

Afternoon: Felt energetic.
Wet things flapped against
my nose on my way to the back door.

Got rid of them.

Demanded oats AND carrots.
Only had to bash the garbage bin
for five minutes before they arrived.

Evening: Have decided that humans
are easily trained and make quite good pets.

Night: Dug new hole
to be closer to them.

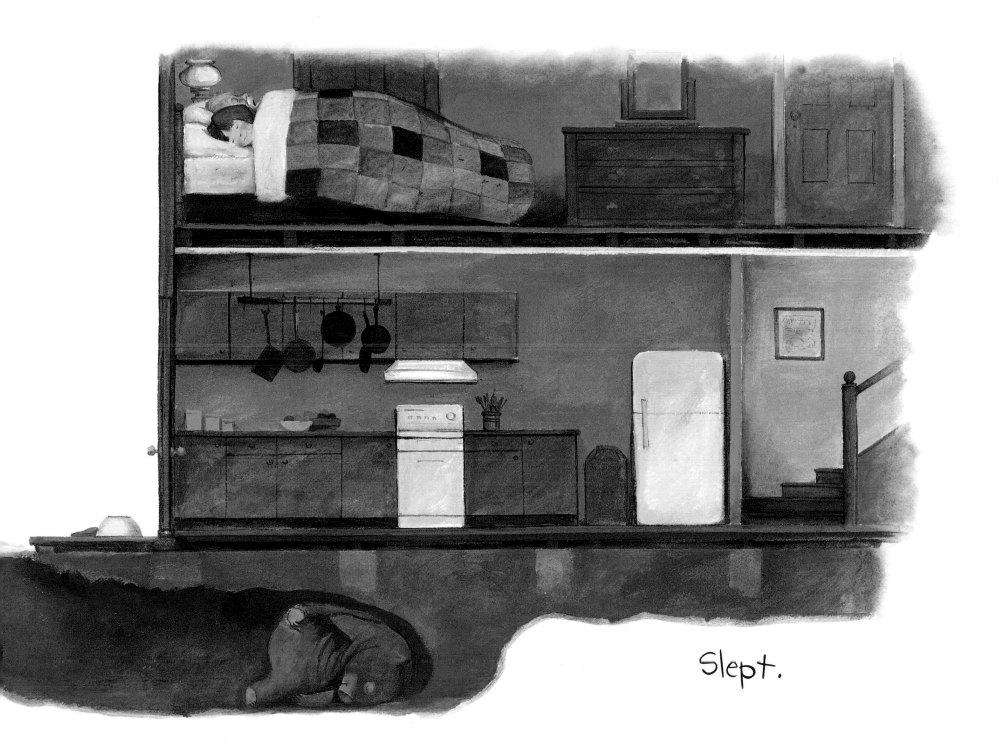

Slept.